If You're So Smart, How Come You Can't Spell Mississippi

WRITTEN BY
BARBARA ESHAM

Little Pickle Press

ILLUSTRATED BY
MIKE AND CARL GORDON

My dad is the smartest person I know.

He is one of the busiest civil rights lawyers
in Chicago, and he works hard to keep justice
in our city.

For the past year, my dad has been getting
ready for a big case.

Have you ever worked on anything for an entire year?

I'm a third grader at Westover Elementary School.
My name is Katie and I'm only eight, but I've been
working on something too.

It's called observation. It's fun because—let me
tell you—I've seen some strange things.

Like the time David, a boy in my class, couldn't resist squeezing the pudding cup from his lunch box.

He had to see how much pressure the lid could take before...well, you know...

And the time my little sister insisted that our family change her name to Eduardo after she finished watching the Cooking with Eduardo show with Grandma.

My little sister is only three years old. I guess she thought it was time for a change.

Just last week I saw Mrs. Higgins driving through town with fourteen Chihuahuas in her car—and those were just the Chihuahuas that I could count as she was passing us.

As you can see, observation is a worthwhile pastime.

But the strangest thing that I have ever observed happened tonight, while I was practicing for my spelling test.

I asked my dad if he could help me with the toughest word on my spelling list: Mississippi. Usually my dad loves to help me, but this time he said, "I'm not sure. Go ask your mom."

"How can you, Dad, one of the smartest people I know, not know how to spell Mississippi?" I asked in astonishment.

"Well, Katie, I never have been a very good speller. In fact, I don't believe that I have ever spelled Mississippi correctly. Actually there are a lot of words I've never spelled correctly," he answered.

"That is the strangest thing that I have heard, Dad, even stranger than Eduardo!" I replied. "How did you make it through the third grade if you couldn't spell Mississippi?"

"Well, it wasn't easy. I was often ashamed of not being able to spell the words on my spelling tests.

In fact, some of my classmates even made fun of me," he said with a serious smile.

"Dad, do you mean that you were kind of like Mark Twingle? He sits in front of me and he can't spell anything!"

"I guess I was like Mark Twingle," he said. "It's tough when you're the kid in the class who works extra hard and still has trouble. I had to spend so much more time on my homework than my sister spent on hers. I would still come home with a C- on my spelling test, and that was on a good day."

"Oooohhhhh, that's terrible," I replied. It was terrible—
and also confusing. I mean, my dad is smart.

"Learning to read was just as difficult," said my dad.
"I was the last kid in my class to learn how to read.
Sometimes I would hide my head when my teacher
would ask me to read to the class."

"Just like Mark does!" I shouted.

How could this be? My dad
was just like Mark Twingle?

This information did not
make sense.

"Katie, we have talked about dyslexia before, remember? Dyslexia is a word used to describe the difficulty that some people experience with reading and spelling, like me," he said after looking over my math homework.

"But Dad, how do you do your job? How can you be so smart if you can't spell or read very well?" I asked.

"Katie, dyslexia does not mean a person isn't smart. In fact, some of the greatest scientists, doctors, and inventors struggled with symptoms of dyslexia," my dad said with a chuckle.

Now, I've observed many strange things, but could it be true that Mark Twingle is the next great mind of our time? Is this possible?

I would need to do a little investigating before I was convinced.

On Saturday, I asked my mom to take me to the public library.

I'm a whiz at the library and it didn't take long to find a book about dyslexia.

It included a list of people throughout history who struggled with reading or spelling. But I'm confused.

Now that we know about dyslexia, why is this still a secret? Why hasn't anyone ever mentioned it in school?

Like this guy: Dr. John R. Skoyles. He works as a neuroscience researcher.

One of his book reports is titled, "The Aetioloy of Autism: Neuroembryology and Prefrontal Neocerebellum." Whoa! He researches things I can't even pronounce! Where is the librarian when you need her the most?

I guess I'll learn about that in fifth grade.

I turned the page to read about Archer J.P. Martin,
a chemist who won the Nobel Prize in 1952.
Fortunately the librarian walked by.

"Mrs. Meeks, can you help me read this? Some of
the words are a little big," I asked quietly.

"Sure. I love to see children reading
on the weekends," she said.

"Let's see here," said Mrs. Meeks.
"Archer Martin's experiments include the discovery
of a method for detecting pyroelectricity by...

"...observing the attraction of a metal plate of crystals that had been immersed in liquid air. Katie, do you need this information for a book report?" she asked with a puzzled look on her face.

"No, no, Mrs. Meeks, I am just doing a little bit of investigating."

Detecting pyroelectricity in liquid air? Is anyone following me on this one?

"Do you want me to keep reading?" Mrs. Meeks asked.

"Oh yes, please," I replied with my most polite voice. I needed help to get through this book.

"Helen B. Tausig was a doctor in the 1930s. Many women at that time didn't even have a chance to go to college, but Helen Tausig studied to become a pediatric cardiologist. She helped discover a new way to help babies who were born with heart problems. She was the first woman to become a full professor at Johns Hopkins University and she was elected president of the American Heart Association."

"She was really smart!" I said.

"I have to go help some other children now, Katie.
Do you think you can take it from here?" asked Mrs. Meeks.

"I'll give it a try," I replied. "If Helen Tausig had trouble reading and writing and she could become a pediatric cardiologist, well I guess I can try to read this book on my own."

Let's see. William James was a psychologist—one of the greatest psychologists of all time.

It looks like he had a lot of interesting things to say. A few of them are right here, in this book.

"I don't sing because I am happy, I am happy because I sing."

"Act as if what you do makes a difference. It does."

"Every good worth possessing must be paid for in strokes of daily effort."

Hey! My dad has this quote framed!
He keeps it on the wall for
everyone to notice...

"Do every day or two something for no other reason than its difficulty."

The names of so many amazing people are in this book and it would take a long time to read all of them.

I guess a lot of people who have trouble with reading and writing, and maybe math too, go on to accomplish great things: writers, architects, scientists, entrepreneurs, actors, artists, athletes, presidents, doctors, lawyers, inventors, college professors, teachers, and even school principals.

BOOKS MAKE YOU SMART

I wonder if my teacher, Mrs. Peterson, knows about dyslexia and all these great people.

I have a feeling that most of these great people had someone to help them through the tough times, when they might have been feeling frustrated or sad.

Maybe their parents were patient and supported them.

Maybe they had a teacher who could see how smart they were anyway.

Maybe the classmate sitting next to them didn't make them feel bad for not being the fastest reader or the best speller.

Now I know why my dad likes what William
James had to say so long ago...

"Do every day or two something for
no other reason than its difficulty."

Is this what people who struggle with dyslexia
tell themselves each day before school?

Did my dad say this to himself through the tough times, when he was trying his best to learn to read and spell?

I can't wait to go to school on Monday.

I think Mark Twingle needs to know how great his mind is and what incredible things he might accomplish one day...

Maybe, I'm just the right person to tell him.

~~The End~~

Just the beginning...

Are YOU an EVERYDAY GENIUS too?

Everyday geniuses are **creative,** STRONG, **thoughtful,**
and sometimes learn a little differently from others.
And that's what makes them so special!

In *If You're So Smart, How Come You Can't Spell Mississippi?*, Katie learns that her dad has dyslexia. She has a hard time understanding how someone so smart and successful can have a learning disability. But her dad's stories and Katie's research prove that a learning disability doesn't mean you can't succeed.

But what is dyslexia? Dyslexia is usually described as a learning disability that is *neurobiological*. This means that dyslexia has to do with a person's nervous system, which includes the brain. Dyslexia often causes difficulty with spelling, recognizing words, and decoding text. It's not just about reversing letters, as many believe.

We saw in this story that Katie's dad struggled with spelling, but his other academic abilities were strong. Having dyslexia did not mean he wasn't smart.

Have you ever struggled to learn something? What happened?

Every person with dyslexia has his or her own best way to help them. If you or someone you know has been diagnosed with dyslexia, you may have tried one or more modifications.

Here are a few examples of modifications people have used in classrooms:

- Listen to audio versions of your books or textbooks to go along with your reading
- Cover up the text on a page so only one line of text is visible at a time
- Use large-type textbooks or handouts of whatever is being read in class

There is no right or wrong method because every person is unique and learns differently. Even if you do not have dyslexia, try using one of these reading accommodations. Do you see the words differently? Do you remember the information you're reading differently?

In the story, Katie's dad says he was teased by other kids for having dyslexia. What are some ways you can help someone who has dyslexia? If you or someone you know has ever struggled with reading or reading comprehension, talk about it with a caring adult.

Remember, it's never a bad thing to be different—embracing and learning from our differences is what makes the world a better place!

Endorsements and Reviews for
THE ADVENTURES OF EVERYDAY GENIUSES

"**This is a wonderful book series.** Each story shows children that success is about effort and determination, that problems need not derail them, and that adults can understand their worries and struggles. My research demonstrates that these lessons are essential for children."

—Dr. Carol S. Dweck, Stanford University
professor of psychology

Carol Dweck is the author of Mindset: The New Psychology of Success. *Her scholarly book* Self-Theories: Their Role in Motivation, Personality, and Development *was named Book of the Year by the World Education Fellowship. Dr. Dweck is one of the world's leading researchers in the field of motivation and is the Virginia Eaton Professor of Psychology at Stanford University.*

"**I applaud Barbara Esham** for finding a way to teach young children how to be more mindful. In so doing, she sets the stage for their greater well-being as adults."

—Dr. Ellen Langer, Harvard University
professor of psychology

"**Over the years I have witnessed great advances** in our understanding of learning styles. Yet I have been struck with how little progress we have made in translating this research into words and practices that students and their parents can use. The books of the Adventures of Everyday Geniuses series are honest but positive, helpful without preaching, and they are readable but not too simplistic. I have no doubt these books will touch the hearts and minds of many, and help some lost children find good in themselves."

—Dr. Jeffrey Gilger, Purdue University,
College of Education Professor and Associate Dean
for Research and Faculty Development

"**In recent years there has been a growing awareness** among educators, researchers, and members of many professions that challenges in reading and spelling are often accompanied by special abilities in areas like complex pattern recognition and spatial reasoning. *If You're So Smart, How Come You Can't Spell Mississippi?* is a fantastic way of bringing this information to the many smart children who find reading and spelling especially difficult—and especially to those who are beginning to doubt their own potential."

—Drs. Brock (M.D., M.A.) and Fernette (M.D.) Eide,
learning experts and physicians consultants to a wide range
of parent, teacher, and clinical professional groups

FOR MORE ENDORSEMENTS, REVIEWS, RESOURCES, AND EVEN LESSON PLANS, PLEASE VISIT
JABBERWOCKYKIDS.COM

About the Author

Author Barbara Esham was one of those kids who couldn't resist performing a pressure test on a pudding cup. She has always been a "free association" thinker, finding life far more interesting while in a state of abstract thought. Barbara lives on the East Coast with her three daughters. Together, in Piagetian fashion, they have explored the ideas and theories behind the definitions of intelligence, creativity, learning, and success. Barb researches and writes from her home office, in the spare time available between car pools, homework, and bedtime.

About the Illustrators

Cartooning has brought Mike Gordon acclaim in worldwide competitions, adding to his international reputation as a top humorous illustrator. Since 1993 he has continued his successful career based in California, gaining a nomination in the prestigious National Cartoonist Society Awards. Mike is the renowned illustrator for the wildly popular book series beginning with *Do Princesses Wear Hiking Boots?* Mike collaborates with his son Carl Gordon from across the world. They have been a team since 1999. Mike creates the line illustrations, and the color is applied by Carl using a graphics tablet and computer. Carl has a degree in graphic art and currently lives in Cape Town, South Africa with his wife and kids.

Copyright © 2013 by Barbara Esham
Cover and internal design © 2018 by Sourcebooks, Inc.
Text by Barbara Esham
Illustrations by Mike and Carl Gordon

Sourcebooks and the colophon are registered trademarks of Sourcebooks, Inc.

The story text was set in OpenDyslexic, a font specifically designed for readability with dyslexia.
The back matter was set in Adobe Garamond Pro.

Published by Little Pickle Press, an imprint of Sourcebooks Jabberwocky
P.O. Box 4410, Naperville, Illinois 60567-4410
(630) 961-3900
Fax: (630) 961-2168
sourcebooks.com

Source of Production: Leo Paper, Heshan City, Guangdong Province, China
Date of Production: February 2018
Run Number: 5011334

Printed and bound in China.
LEO 10 9 8 7 6 5 4 3 2 1

THE ADVENTURES ∗F EVERYDAY GENIUSES